Johnny the Story of a Doll

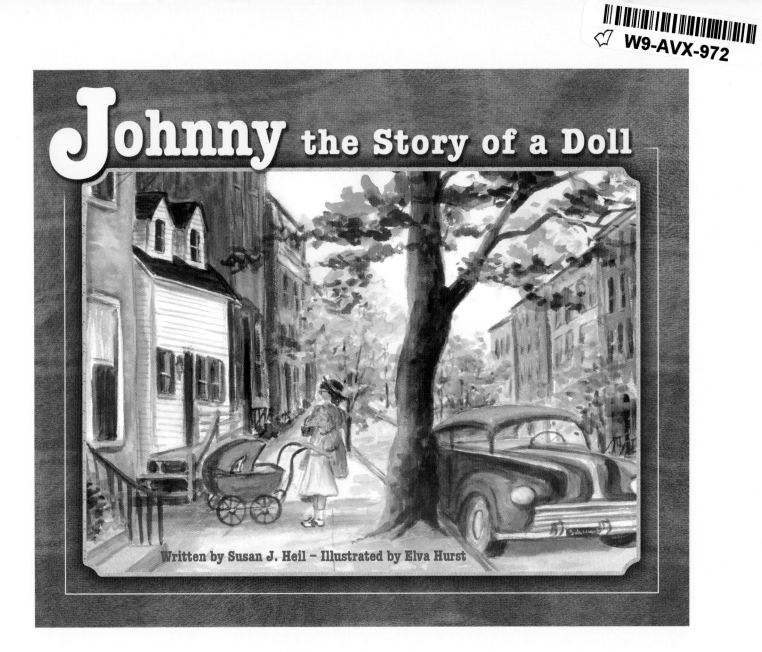

Written by Susan J. Heil – Illustrated by Elva Hurst

Silver Line
PUBLISHING and BINDERY LLC

Johnny, The Story of a Doll

ISBN 978-0-615-50416-2

Printed in the USA

First Printing 2011

Publishing Services By:
Silverline Publishing and Bindery LLC
510 Sleepy Hollow Road, Lititz, PA 17543

To order more books or write to Johnny, mail to:
Sue's Books
PO Box 13
Strasburg, PA 17579

In Memory of...

Uncle John, who gave me Johnny
&
my dear mother, who taught me to appreciate all things old and beautiful.

Dedicated to...

my loving husband, who just happens to be named John.

Acknowledgements

Cora Anne Hurst and The Village Doll Hospital Blue Ball, Pennsylvania operated by "Doctor" Kay Raffensperger

Foreword

George Erisman, better known as Uncle George, after working with his father, touring with a band, learning to repair watches, and having several other work experiences in Lancaster, Pennsylvania, opened a doll hospital in a log frame building at 315 West Orange Street in 1908. He maintained a business there for over 50 years repairing dolls and renting costumes.

Shortly after Mr. Erisman's death in 1961, at the age of 97, the doll hospital was sold at a public auction.

The property was purchased by the Covenant EUB Church next door. The Erisman family home was torn down for a

Erisman House at
Museum 2011

parking lot and "the frame-over-log" doll hospital building was given to the Pennsylvania Farm Museum of Landis Valley. At that time the building was estimated to be 150-200 years old. It consisted of four rooms on the first floor and two rooms and a storage area on the second floor. The log work was said to be dove-tailed.

In 1963, the doll hospital took a very slow 5 mph trip through Lancaster City on a big flatbed truck to its new home on the property of the Landis Valley Farm Museum, a few miles outside the city limits. The building stands today at the museum as The Erisman House. It is open to the public and maintained as the home of an early seamstress.

Johnny, The Story of a Doll

written by

Susan J. Heil

illustrated by

Elva Hurst

My doll's name is Johnny.
When I was little he was
so big that it was hard for me
to carry him.

My mommy made Johnny
lots of clothes. Johnny and
I liked the matching yellow
corduroy hat and overalls the
best.

Johnny was big enough to wear real baby clothes too. Sometimes he would wear clothes I had once worn when I was a baby.

Johnny didn't like to wear dresses or bonnets.

My mommy had lovingly kept my baby clothes in a
large tin lard can in the attic.

When Johnny needed a new outfit we would go
shopping in the can.

He wore one of my shirts with his yellow overalls
and the hat that Mommy made for him.

11

Johnny went everywhere with me.
He liked to visit Grandma's house
best because she had a swing on her
porch and lots of pretty flowers.

Sometimes Grandma would give us a snack. Johnny liked the peanut butter crackers, but I liked the sugar bread best.

Sometimes we would pretend to go on long trips.

Sometimes we would play nurse.

Sometimes we would play dress up.

Sometimes we would play school.

Sometimes Johnny
and I had a tea party.
We invited friends.

Because Johnny was so big
and I was so little, I would drop
him often and his eyes would fall
back into his head. I would cry.
Mommy and I would have to go
to the doll hospital in Lancaster
with Johnny.

Mommy, Johnny, and I would walk to the bus stop.
If it was cold outside we would wait inside the gas
station so we could stay warm. I liked the special smell of
the gas station.

I would always look at the ice cream treats so
I could tell Daddy just what to bring home for
me the next time he went to the gas station.

21

We liked the bus ride to Lancaster very much.

In Lancaster we had to walk to the doll hospital from the bus stop. I liked to look at the pretty hats and grown-up shoes in the store windows. Mommy called that window shopping.

If we were lucky, we would see the soft pretzel man and Mommy would buy us some for the ride home on the bus.

25

I was afraid of the steps at the doll hospital. I thought they were steep and I could see through the backs of them.

I was glad to get inside and see the doctor, Mr. Erisman. He liked Mommy, Johnny, and me. He had big pockets in his apron where he kept licorice drops for his visitors.

He would examine Johnny carefully and then take him into the room behind the curtain.

When he returned, Johnny was all fixed up.

On one of our trips to see Mr. Erisman a sad thing happened. I fell down those scary steps and dropped Johnny after he was all fixed up and ready to go home. His eyes fell right back in his head again!

I cried. Mommy was frustrated. Johnny looked scared.

Johnny went home from the hospital that day in the same condition in which he had arrived. His eyes were still rattling around in his head. We could not take him back into the hospital to see Mr. Erisman again that day. Mommy said we would be late for the bus home if we took Johnny back inside. So, she gave us both a Band-Aid to make us feel better.

As I grew into a young lady, Johnny and I made many more trips to Mr. Erisman's Doll Hospital.

Johnny and I played together for many years. When I grew up and went to live in a home of my own, Johnny and my other dolls were moved to the attic for safe keeping.

Over the years while Johnny was in the attic his body aged and he lost his stuffing. He was sad and lonely because I no longer played with him.

Not that long ago I went into Mommy's attic and found Johnny. Mommy knew how much I loved Johnny. She must have found him in his sorry state and carefully placed him in a chest to keep him safe.

His head was safely wrapped in his yellow corduroy overalls. With a little searching in the chest, I found his cap and his favorite little shirt.

It was a cold winter's day that I again carried Johnny into another doll hospital.

I was told Johnny would be as good as new in a few short weeks if I could be patient enough to wait until a donor body could be located.

I was so excited when I got the news that I could bring Johnny home from the hospital.

I took Johnny home
wrapped in a baby
blanket to keep him safe.
I carried him very
carefully. I did not want
to slip on the ice and drop
him.

When we got inside
I sat Johnny on a rocking
chair by the Christmas
tree. My nana had given
me the rocking
chair many
Christmases ago.

Johnny will always have a special place in my home and in my heart.

Author's Note

The Erisman Doll Hospital, as well as the Mr. George Frederick Krotel Erisman (1863-1961), are considered local treasures in Lancaster, Pennsylvania. Such treasures, made and continue to make our country great. They need to be remembered by the generations that follow them. Everyday people are what we use as role models and whose stories we need to pass on to our children. Not so long ago a toy was treasured for life, not just thrown on a garage sale pile when a new one would replace it in a wasteful moment of temptation for something new, bigger, or better. We are a society that discards the old, be it an old doll or an elderly person. How wise we would be to care for them, love them, and listen to the stories they have to tell.

The sheer joy of memories that flood back when we pick up a childhood toy or listen to an older person telling stories of their past is precious. Taking time to treasure things and people is becoming lost in a world that moves forward too fast with little regard for where it came from. Little children learned to be good mothers caring for their dolls. Maybe I learned to be more frugal because my mother took me to a doll hospital rather than a local store for a new doll when my doll needed repair. Every time I look at Johnny he helps me remember many of the important things in my life. I can share my stories with my grandchild when he asks why Johnny is always under the Christmas tree. The shop owner on the corner, the lady next door, and you, are living lives of purpose. Share your lives and stories before a generation slips by unnoticed and unappreciated.

Mr. Erisman, in a interview with a Lancaster newspaper in 1954, commented that he didn't understand why all the fuss about him. His simple life, by many standards, reached the hearts of countless children. Their stories of the memories he created for them are found in the archives of the Lancaster County Historical Society, Lancaster Newspapers, and the city library's microfiche. Memory stories are personally rewarding in the telling and often inspiring to others.

I am grateful for my memories of Mr. Erisman that have inspired me to write this book. Hopefully, *Johnny, The Story of a Doll* will inspire others to cherish their memories. Future generations can thus learn from their stories and be inspired also to notice and live simple lives of purpose.